A Sweater for Duncan

Written by Margaret Gay Malone

Illustrated by Lorraine Dey

To Connor Robert and Mackenzie Elizabeth, with love – MGM

In loving memory of my mother, Joan.
To my nephews and nieces, Jeremy, Kelly, Natalie, Noelle, Theresa, and Joe.
Thanks to Dona for support and encouragement. – LD

Text ©2010 by Margaret Gay Malone
Illustration ©2010 by Lorraine Dey

Malone, Margaret Gay.

    A sweater for Duncan / written by Margaret Gay Malone; illustrated by Lorraine Dey;
    —1st ed. —McHenry, IL: Raven Tree Press, 2010.

    p. ; cm.

    SUMMARY: The little penguin is proud of his fuzzy coat. When his fuzz starts to fall off,
        he wants a sweater, until he discovers he's become a grown up penguin.

English Edition
ISBN 978-1-936299-06-5 hardcover

Bilingual Edition
ISBN 978-1-936299-04-1 hardcover
ISBN 978-1-936299-05-8 paperback

    Audience: pre-K to 3rd grade
    Title available in English-only or bilingual English-Spanish editions

    1. Animals / Marine Life—Juvenile fiction. 2. Social Issues / Self-Esteem &
    Self-Reliance—Juvenile fiction. I. Illust. Dey, Lorraine. II. Title.

LCCN: 2010922815

Printed in Taiwan
10 9 8 7 6 5 4 3 2 1
First Edition

Free activities for this book are available at www.raventreepress.com

Raven Tree Press
A Division of Delta Systems Co., Inc.
www.raventreepress.com

Duncan the penguin was a fine looking fellow.
He wore a soft coat of gray fuzz, not like most penguins.
They looked like they wore a black coat and a white shirt.

At least once every day, he admired his reflection in a piece of ice as shiny as glass. He liked what he saw. He'd stick out his chest and waddle proudly among the other penguins.
He knew he was the handsomest.

One day a piece of fluff floated to his feet.
He looked down at his tummy and right where
the fluff should be, was a small bare spot.
He scooped up the piece and pressed
it into his tummy. As soon as he let go,
the fluff floated to the ground.
"One little spot isn't bad," he thought.

When he woke up the next morning, two more tufts lay in the snow. The little spot grew to a medium spot. The medium spot grew to a big spot.

8

When the wind blew, he had to chase another clump of fuzz. He slid down a snowy hill as it skipped ahead in the wind. Duncan caught a wingful of fuzz. He had to do something.

"Mother," he said, "I used to be a fine looking fellow.
Will you make me a sweater to cover my bare spots?"
"With whatever fuzz falls off,
I'll make you a sweater," mother said.
Duncan hugged his mother. "Thank you."

12

13

Every day, the wind howled in icy gusts. Duncan huffed after the tufts that flew off his body like butterflies. He'd pounce on them as they tumbled along, and take them to his mother.

Finally, she held up a sweater.
"Try this on." He tried to button it.
"Too tight," he said, disappointed.
A few days later, he tried on a
bigger one. "Too short," he said,
tugging at the sleeves.

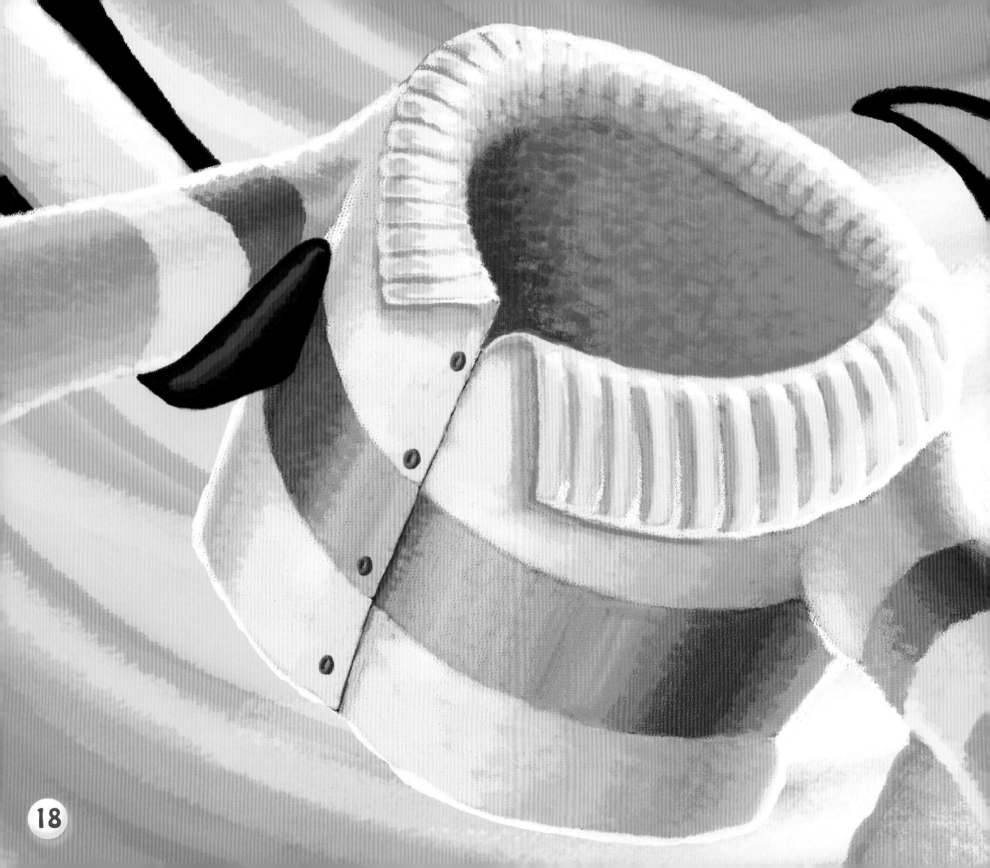

One day, his mother handed him a bigger
sweater. "Don't try it on yet," she said.
"First, I have a surprise for you."
His mother led him to a familiar spot.
It was the glassy ice where
Duncan used to admire himself.

"What's my surprise?" Duncan asked.
"Look at yourself."
Duncan didn't want to look. He stood in front
of the ice-mirror with his eyes shut tight.
"Go on," his mother said.

Duncan opened one eye, then the other. He was looking at a tall, grown up penguin. He wore feathers that looked like a white shirt and a black coat. Could it be? His mother nodded. "It's you."

This time, Duncan took a long look.
He had turned into a grownup, and
quite a handsome one.
"Mother, you knew!" Duncan said.

25

Mother smiled. "What do you want me to do with the sweater?"

27

"Whatever you want," Duncan answered. "I like what I see."

"I don't need it, now that I'm a fine looking, grown up fellow."